Treading Water

A Syllble Studios Collaboration

By David Russell and Josh Eiermann

Syllble Studios

Table of Contents

The Beginning

After the Great Manufacturing Boom in the 1960s, the air outside became a dense, toxic smog that resulted in a dull burn with every breath someone took. For the first time in Earth's recent history, the life expectancy stopped increasing, and slowly started to reverse. People grew tired of breathing through a gas mask, which wasn't cheap. The wealthy were able to install air filtration to keep their home free of toxins, but the poor, they were out of luck.

Much of the low-income population died of respiratory issues. As inflation became widespread, a growing number of middle-class and even some of the wealthy population struggled to afford survival. Protesting led to rioting, and suddenly, the governments of the world were racing to find a solution to ensure the survival of the human race.

Developed countries looked to space. A few planets were found to be suitable for colonization, but ultimately, the atmosphere would require artificial habitats. At a time when sea-levels were swallowing cities whole, underdeveloped countries began taking these habitats developed for space, and simply putting them underwater. Although the design of each underwater habitat was similar, it was up to individual countries and local governments to make the transition. Some governments were successful, others not so much.

Teams that worked efficiently were successful, but humans were humans, and toxic individuals could ruin a community. Piza fell into a category of his own. He prefered to do things alone. Although, he wasn't toxic to the community *yet*, word was that you could smell how toxic Piza really was.

Piza's First Drug Run

by Josh Eiermann

"I desperately need a drink if I'm going to be stuck underwater with these people for the rest of my life."

SHRMP conveniently chimed in, "alcohol production is at an all-time low, nearly zero, but water is healthy and you can drink it."

Piza scoffed under his breath, "For fuck's sake, I *live* in the water."

However, the talk of trade with other underwater communities gave Piza hope. Communities specialized in production of different goods, but Piza had figured out a way to produce most basic goods with his customized habitat. To most, these basic goods of meat and plants was enough. To Piza, and a handful of others, drugs and alcohol were also a necessity.

"SHRMP, how long would it take to get us to Panama City?"

"About 17 minutes to Panama City Beach," SHRMP said with a strained voice, trying not to giggle knowing he meant the *other* Panama City.

Piza's eyes turned white, rolling back into his head as he rephrased his question: "SHRMP, how long would it take to get us to Panama City, *Panama*?"

"About 3 hours and 12 minutes."

The Panama Canal was once the trade gateway for the West and the East. Now, much of the country is submerged except for the mountainous region, but still acts as a pathway through the Americas. Most of the country's income came from the canal.

"SHRMP, can you run a query on my connections and find out if any of them have gone through Panama lately?"

"Cookie and Wilson."

Piza sighs, "Call Cookie please."

"HEY MY PIZA PIE FACE!" Cookie enthusiastically belts into the phone.

Piza cringes, "Please stop… anyway, I heard you went on a trade run recently, did you travel through Panama? If so, how was it?"

"Let's just say I travelled through it as quick as the ship could possibly go. Their community is struggling and shady people run the place now."

"What kind of goods are they trading? Anything useful?" Piza curiously, and not so subtly questioned.

"The kinds of goods that get you killed."

This was exactly the answer that Piza wanted. He wasn't looking for cows, he was looking for cashcows. Piza's ship alone had everything Panama's habitat needed: rice, beans, beef, and herbs. Panama possibly had drugs and alcohol, and if Piza were to go rogue and trade directly with Panama instead of providing the food to his Miami community, he could make massive profits. Piza dreamed of a world where he was self-sustainable and far from the annoying characters in Miami (or anywhere, really).

Piza was essentially sitting on an invention that could sustain the world. His mini habitat had climate control that would allow him to farm 90% of the food variety that existed in the previous world. Piza could tell communities about this technology but he fails to see how he can benefit from that. "I could license it out and get paid royalties," he usually contemplates, but his lack of trust in *the system* silences this idea. Regardless, if anyone knew he was sitting on the technology that could save entire communities or give them autonomous power, pirates would be there immediately.

"Trading food off the books is the same as trading drugs, so it's a perfectly fair trade, and there are tons of people willing to get drugs lowkey, so I can push them quickly with minimal attention."

Piza had it all figured out.

"SHRMP, I'm going to volunteer to do a trade run soon, but I'm going to need your help."

"You always need my help, human."

"You don't even have thumbs SHRMP," Piza slowly stretching his middle fingers to the sky, "I'll need you to break the ship down in Panama.

"That seems like a bad place to be stuck, Piza. I would rather breakdown in Hawaii or India."

Piza, growing impatient and frustrated, refuses to entertain the banter and instead opens a spreadsheet. He spends the next few hours calculating the possible profits. He slams the computer shut to reveal a glowing smile and bloodshot eyes.

In an obnoxiously loud declaration, Piza shouts "the first thing I'm   buying   is   a   new   AI   system."

Piza goes to Miami

By David Russell

CRUNCH, BANG, SPLASH. The entire cabin jerks forward knocking Piza's clock off his desk. *Looks like those idiots finally made their way out of a paper bag into the water.*

Intercom,"We have now breached the ocean, we expect to land into Miami at 1300 hours". *I miss the good ole' days where I could just drive there myself.* "All members of the ship must report to the Town Hall at 0900 hours". *Fantastic, another waste of time.*

"SHRMP, grab my glasses. I still have hours of work to do in the hull before we can get the fuck out of here." says Piza. "Which ones asshole?" says S.H.R.M.P. (Ship Helper Robot Miniature Prosthesis). "...the clear ones. Now's not the time, in fact it's never a good time for you to talk." SHRMP hovers over to the bed, scoops up the specs and throws them across the room over to Piza's lap. *I wish I knew what an "entertaining" droid meant when I requested mine.* "Okay Pizza, you have your glasses now. Shall we go, or do I need to carry you?" *That'd be nice.*

Piza stands up in his blank white room with open pipes stringing along the roof and the walls. He places his hand on the wall's hand scanner and the door slides open. *They never clean the engineering bay, they think just because we are hard of sight we can't see all the shit on the walls.* He makes his way down the corridor into the elevator when he notices a new flyer. *Join us tonight for a night of prayer and repentance as we embark in this new world.* *God's left us out to dry a long time ago, I almost feel bad for them..*

The open elevator shaft flew down 20 stories as he looked out to each terminal on the ship. He stopped briefly on level 10, his favorite deck. The cafeteria. "Got anything good for me today?" asks Piza with a brief hint of hope. "Do we ever?" says the Chef Bob. "You are welcome to some of this shit, not even the dogs wanted to finish it." The chef tosses over half of an empty bag of dark green crackers. "What a life, thanks.." says Piza. He walks back toward the elevator and takes a bite of a cracker, gags a bit, but swallows it down. *Out of all the people on this crazy ship, he's the one I might actually miss.*

Piza made his way into the Hull to see the 12 ship fleet he had created. The sum of his life's work. *This is sad. At least I know unit 3 is taking me out of here.* As he walks down the steps onto the hull floor he slips and lands on his back, staring up at the ceiling. *There has got to be something more out there. Something better than this.* "SHRMP, give me the analysis of the fleet," "Everything looks up to speed, except vessel #3." "What?! Elaborate!" "It smells like shit." *Sometimes I think I might be better off without this piece of trash.*

It's time to get to work on the final rigs to vessel 3. I need to apply extra Air bubble dispensers as well as extra thrust to be able to last even an extra month out there alone. Piza makes his way to the equipment bay, scans his hand and takes out the additional parts for his watercraft. *At least there is one perk to being the only architect on this ship.* Time flies by as Piza's dream and ship grow until suddenly his peace is crushed.

Intercom, "It is now 0850 hours, everyone on board MUST report to the town hall immediately. That is all." *If he gives another speech about how we all are one moving into this new world, I swear.*

"Welcome new Miamians, as you know we are all one moving into this new world." Captain Polar orates to a massive set of stadium seats facing the main deck of the ship as thousands look on. "We have all been working hard for the last 10 years preparing for these coming moments, and the time has finally come. As our leadership has explained, for our first months upon landing we will all need to work double time to ensure a smooth transition to our new city."

"DOUBLE TIME? WE ARE ALREADY STRETCHED THIN! I'VE BARELY MET MY SON!" yelled a man from the crowd, who was promptly escorted out of the stands.

"Yes, we know you all have, but we just ask for your trust this one more time." Captain Polar says, as his gold encrusted jacket shimmers in the light on the stage. "I promise you once we re-establish Miami, we can open up trade with the other communities and we will all receive endless bounties for our hard work." Some members of the audience cheer and applaud. *The overseers, the laziest of us all.* "In roughly 6 more hours, our lives will change forever when we land above Brickle. It will take at least another week for our air globules to expand and we can begin excavating the ruins. But tonight, we celebrate! Everyone will receive a free sugar packet in their rooms tonight with their food rations. Don't eat it all in one bite!" more cheers erupt from the crowd. *So this is what we have been reduced to.* "We will be making one more announcement upon arrival, you are all excused to leave. Officers, please follow our escorts into the command room for further discussion."

The crowd begins shifting back into the corridors. Captain Polar gestures the officers and overseers who remain to follow him forward underneath the stage. *This ought to be good.* Polar guides them into a circular room with screens displaying security footage from inside and around the ship. They all take seats on the plush purple chairs facing each other on the circular table.

"Ladies and Gentlemen, this is the moment we have all been waiting for. Once we touch ground we will need to make sure our people stay in order and do not explore too far on their own. There is much to explore, and we are largely unfamiliar with the area. We will have our own task force scout the buildings first to make sure there are no pressing dangers." *Dangers? HA! You slimy son of a bitch just want to claim any relics you find for yourself. Me too.* "Leeroy, Adams, you will scout Brickle. Amy, Veronica, you will scout South Beach. Piza, you just make sure our ships work so we don't have the same issues that saw your parents die." Leeroy and Adams share a fiendish chuckle. *These guys are lucky I'm stuck in here, for now.* "As for the rest of you, keep our people entertained. We want this new transition to the floor be as smooth as possible. Let's make it happen." says Captain Polar as he curtly stands up and walks out of the room.

"We better not have any problems here Pizza, or I might just have to take your things myself." sneers Leeroy. "Yeah, what he said." says Adams. *I wouldn't be surprised if these two got lost and died inside their own cruiser, dumbasses.* "I heard Polar, your ships are ready. Make sure to press the 'On' button to start the cruisers." says Piza. Leeroy and Adams give him a nasty glare and bump his shoulder on the way out of the room. Amy and Veronica shrug, and also make their leave. *Yeah, fuck this place.*

Piza made his way back up to his corridor to catch a hint of rest before the landing. His head hits the pillow, eyes heavy. Seemingly moments after closing his eyes red lights ignite the room, followed by a blaring horn that echoes through the hallways. The intercom kicks in, "We've landed!"

Piza's Bad Trip

By David Russell

It feels like an eternity since we've landed on the sea floor, but it's only been a week. "SHRMP, how much longer can I take living in this place?" asks Piza sarcastically. "I'm surprised you haven't died here yet." says SHRMP. *Stupid thing might actually have a point.* Intercom, "Calling all officers, please report to Mission Control for your weekly briefing." Piza sits up on the side of his bed, combs his straight brown hair, and rubs the crust away from his silver eyes. *I'll be out of here soon enough. Where are those green crackers...*

"There were red ones! And blue ones! And Oran-" "that's ENOUGH Amy." Captain Polar says sternly. "I need to know what nutrients you've found in the buildings. Our food rations will only last two months. We NEED to find a sustainable plant to feed our cattle." Polar turns to look at Leeroy, "Please tell me you two have made something useful of your trip."

"Sorry Captain, we didn't find anything." says Leeroy as he breaks eye contact with Polar to stare at his feet. Adams follows suit. *These guys must be some of the worst liars on the planet.* Captain Solar slams his fist on the table, "Do you take me for a fucking idiot? We have surveillance on all of your ships. I saw you enter the Marina, and collect that algae. Next thing I know you are laughing hysterically and sleeping on the job." Polar's diamond glasses sparkle as his eyes narrow to a glare. "People on this ship are starving, and all you two can think about is getting high?" *Psychedelic algae? Sounds fun, and lucrative.* "Piza please for the love of god, give me some good news about the ships." "All crafts are operating, and I've installed the high capacity engines on the interceptors." say Piza. "Wow, I cannot believe I am saying this, but nice work officer, for a pizza that is." *Man I'd love to see your face when these goons try to come after me in their busted crafts.* "I've had enough with you all, leave me." *Gladly, time to pay good old Chef Bob a visit.*

"We have dehydrated chicken and fish spaghetti!" Chef Bob yells to the line of sorry saps waiting for the trough. "I'll take the fish spaghetti, throw me an extra salt pack if you can." says Piza. "No can do friend, I like you, but not that much." *Okay I won't miss him.*

"This stuff is great, you've gotta try some later Amy!" says Leeroy as he discreetly opens a small sachel under the cafeteria table. *The whole damn mess hall can hear these idiots.* "Do you think there is more?" asks Amy. "Oh yea, we saw a massive trail of this stuff getting larger and larger about a mile South." says Leeroy. "We are going to cut the wires on our cameras and go out for more tomorrow. We'll just blame the cut wires on the architect." *We'll see about that.*

Piza finishes his gruel, and runs back up to his quarters. "SHRMP, it's time to go." "Now? But I just started sleeping 10 hours ago.." "Yes, now." Piza rushed around his room, scooping up a bag full of his belongings. 4 pairs of clothes, protein bars, and a laptop. He threw it all into his bag and took one last look at his room. *It's go time.*

Before he could leave, he knew he would need to disable the cameras in his ship. Dim lights from the floors crossed his face as he rode the elevator down to the bay. No one gave him a second glance. He made his way over to his modified craft and put his belongings inside the hatch. Seconds after he unplugged the camera, he heard the Intercom, "There has been a breach in the engineering bay. Security, bring Piza to me." Piza's heart went from racing to light speed as he jumped out of his craft and ran over to the interceptors. He quickly cut the wires to their cameras and batteries. As he gets to his chair and hits the deploy button he sees the elevator door open to expose Leeroy and Adams, "STOP RIGHT THERE PIZZA. YOU'RE IN FUCKING TROUBLE NOW!" Sirens and red lights blaring in the bay as his craft slowly lowers into the departure tunnel. "We're almost home free SHRMP!" suddenly the bay door stops half way open. "Shit, shit, shit!" Piza yanks the steering sideways and barely scrapes the vessel through the doors as he plunges deep below the ship. SHRMP, "Those scratches are going to take you forever to fix." *That's one problem I'm okay with worrying about.*

Piza pulls out his map and compass, with all this stress it's time to find that algae. "They said due south of the marina, I suppose we can start there SHRMP."

The dark silver craft hovered over multiple rows of buildings and streets left over from the flooding. "I had ideas of what this place looked like, but I've gotta say this is depressing." "Not as depressing as hearing you talk." replies SHRMP.

"Do you see that over there? I can see a green patch trailing off from the buildings. We must be close." Piza guides the ship just over the sandbank and dips deeper into the water. Thousands of fish swim by, some with huge fins he had never seen before. *Seems like a good enough place to start scouting.* He turns on his ships lights and points them toward the sea floor. Throws on his scuba gear and enters the water. *Let's see.. If I follow where most of the fish are that should be a good sign something will be there.* Piza swims toward a small dip in the sand to see a massive bowl of the algae Leeroy was describing. *This must be how the cowboys felt in California during the gold rush..*

Beaming with joy, he swims down to the plants and starts to harvest some with his clippers and place it into his bag. As he clips the 3rd, or 10th, or 1000th plant he starts to notice his vision blurring and his body beginning to tingle. Soon he can start hearing the fish swimming around him speaking to him. *Could they always speak english?* He looks down at his hands and notices they have begun waving with the current of the ocean. *I'm a fish!* His watch begins beeping which snaps him back to reality *25% oxygen left in your tank*. *Oh shit, I'm tripping hard. This is awesome, I think.. Wait. What was I doing here?* His watch beeps again *20% oxygen left in your tank*. *Let me ask SHRMP what to do.. Where is it? Wait, my ship!* *15% oxygen left in your tank*.

In an erratic panic, Piza begins swimming back up to his ship. By this time all of the water had turned pink, the algae looked like limes, and there was his ship; a bright yellow submarine. He pushed his way through the pink slime being carried along by sea goddess and his new friend Frank the mino. *10%

oxygen left in your tank*. "I love you Frank, but I have to fly away now in my yellow submarine. I'll remember you forever!" He opens the door to his ship, closes the hatch and throws himself onto the floor. Staring up at the ceiling he appreciates the beautiful stars in the sky a.k.a. - the lights in the control room. The whole ship begins to shake. *Wow this stuff is heavy, I'm gonna be rich!* About a minute later, the whole ship shakes again, this time a bit more violently. *That felt a little too real.*

He stands up in his ship to look out the window and sees an enormous shadow swimming around his craft. As it approaches closer, the ships lights reveal a giant turtle 5 times the size of his of his craft lurking outside. Its mouth covered in the lime green algae. "SHRMP, start the engine NOW!" "You mean now like later?" "I mean turn on the fucking engine!" SHRMP turns on the propellers and they begin to propel forward away from Miami. This startles the turtle who dips down underneath the ship creating a vacuum that pulls the ship down with it several hundred feet. "Holy shit, we are dead!" Piza cries out as his final words. The turtle emerges a few meters in front of the window and kicks forward with its humongous legs. The momentum from the swim launches them forward about a mile into a current heading towards the panama canal. He looks around and the turtle is nowhere to be seen. "SHRMP, never trip with people who make you anxious..." *Frank, I know you have it rough out there buddy. Hang in there!*

Piza's Old Friend and New Enemies
By David Russell

"Head due north at that volcano over there, and we should start seeing the island," says Kai. "Simple enough," Piza says pessimistically. They pass their way through the massive mountains spewing lava in route to Honolulu when they first catch site of Mauna Kea. *I've always wondered what these hawaiians had going on.*

Bright lights flash onto their ship, and they hear a sharp horn blast through the water. "It's them," says Kai.. "What?!?! You said this was a safe route!" says Piza. "It WAS, I don't know why they'd be out this far." The intercom on their ship kicks on, "This is the Hawaiian Security patrol, please turn off your engines. We are coming over to inspect your ship."

"Shit. What are the odds we can out run them, Kai?" says Piza.

"Given that they have 100s of ships, and are much faster, I'd say 0 and they might shoot us down."

"Okay then, here we go… we need to hide the algae. SHRMP, take all of the plants and put them inside you!" "I'm not taking one for you." SHRMP says disobediently. "Yes, you are you POS!" Piza opens up SHRMP's chest cavity and stashes the bag. Not a minute later, the security ship attaches its opening to theirs. Up close they could see the ship was 3 times as large, they were stuck. They open the door for them to find a burly man and stern looking woman wearing white and gold uniforms with the Honolulu flag prominently displayed on their chests.

"What order of business do you have crossing into these waters?" the woman says. "We are just a couple of traders, looking to commerce with the islands." says Piza.

"What type of commerce?" the man says, with a hint of frustration on his brow. "I am an engineer and an inventor, I've developed a new proprietary farming technology that will revolutionize how we create food!" the two security guards sense incenserity in Piza's voice. "And what about that little chrome guy over there?" They point over to SHRMP who is trying to hide in the corner. "Oh don't worry about him, he is just a trash can." jests Piza. "Trash Can? Then why are you relying on me to save you? Says SHRMP. *Not now, just shut up!*

The security officers make their way over to shrimp and open up his chest cavity to find the bag of algae. *Oh fuck.* The officers glance at each other and make a call over the intercom. "We have found 2 men just South of Mauna Kea attempting to smuggle contraband into the islands." says the man into his com device, "You know people die from this shit all the time, how dare you try to come in and ruin our people's lives. You two are coming with us." *Yeah, yeah, save the lectures for your children, you don't know me.*

The officers make their way out and attach cords to their ship to taxi them to Honolulu. "Well, at least we don't have to worry about recharging the ship again on our way to the island.." Piza tells Kai. Kai digs his face into his hands and begins to cry. "Do you even know what the prisons are like over there? They put us in cells with the animals, and make us fight them off for food. And that's when they actually give us food!" *Eh, can't be that bad.*

As they get closer to Honolulu, they start to see the incredible architecture of the city. At least 10 kilometer wide air globules fill the area and under there is a bustling city with vehicles, working street lights and people walking about the sidewalks.

"SHRMP, this place is incredible!" says Piza.
"Just wait till you see the inside of the cells.." says Kai.

They make their descent into a sandbank on the northern corner of the island to see a run down globule with a dark grainy floor.

"This is it, get out and don't make any sudden moves." says the burly man. He guides them into the first of 4 rusty barred cells. "Welcome to your new home. Food will be served tomorrow morning."

"Well this isn't so bad, right guys?" says Piza. Kai begins to sob while SHRMP turns off his voice box. *How can we escape?* He glances around the room and notices a few wooden chairs. *Eurica!* Piza picks up the chair and slams it into the rusted bar only to see the chair leg splinter off. *Well, I tried everything..* They hear a door crack open from a few yards away and light pours into the cells.

"A contraband dealer with Kai, and a sarcastic robot?" says an ominous woman's voice. She makes her way to the front of the cage to find her long lost childhood best friend. "Piza?"

"Parm?"

Piza and Parm's Hawaii

By Josh Eiermann

Before the earth went to absolute shit, Hawaii was one of the most beautiful places in the world. Lush forests and volcanoes making the island come alive. The air was so toxic that the trees just went flaccid; the smog so heavy that towering green mountains weren't even visible anymore. The people of Hawaii practically lived in the ocean, so naturally, their habitat was one of the most advanced in the world. Hell, some of them even swam faster than the older personal ships.

"The design, the technology, the - " Piza rambled in awe, jaw grazing the ocean bed. *This is like a sexual experience.* " - this place is incredible!" "If I had eyes, they would be rolling into my head," an eyeless SHRMP mumbled.

Parm was grateful to be home and safe, but she had an uneasy feeling. She was visibly bothered and finally confronted Piza. "You're so smart and resourceful, Piza. Why do you keep that to yourself instead of sharing your engineering gift with the world? Running drugs might be lucrative, but if you haven't noticed, we live in underwater habitats and being rich is useless. Teams survive, not individuals."

Piza's excitement turned to annoyance, "the invention that I have holds a lot of power, and we don't want that kind of power in the wrong hands."

"So you're going to just hold all the power? Got it." At this point, Parm was scheming. She was optimistic that Piza would eventually allow habitats access to his farm technology despite knowing it was a longshot. *If I steal his technology for the benefit of the world- he just needs some time to come around.*

"This place is so shiny," Piza said distracting himself and ignoring Parm's pestering.

A group of friends were talking in the cafeteria and someone blurted out "Did you guys hear about Samoa???" *Oh shit.*

Piza's eyes shifted to the TV: Samoa Looted by Pirates, On the Verge of Sinking.

Samoa was a seriously wealthy habitat. They hired the best people in the area to build their ships, mostly from Hawaii. Expensive items like artwork, statues, and artifacts were housed in their habitat because so many of the estates there collected them. They were a floating target.

"Piza, we have to go help them."
"Fine, let's go."

A couple hours later, Piza and Parm could see Samoa on the horizon. Several of the orbs in their habitat were barely hanging onto the main frame. Trailing behind them were about 100 other ships from Hawaii, enough to shuttle refugees to other cities.

Piza and the Sacred Seed

By David Russell

At least 200 pirates ships were strewn about the orbs of Samoa. Green, red, and white vessels shimmered like ornaments against the plastic walls.

As the Honolulu fleet drew closer, they began to see dark figures running in and out of the buildings with others crouching on the ground with their heads down. As they enter the first orb, a man steps in front of them with a laser and is instantly shot. "Damn Parm, nice shot!" says Piza.
"Stay close, and secure the perimeters. MOVE!" says Parm.

The white and gold members of the Honolulu forces sprint over to two nearby buildings and signal for the rest to follow. They emerge onto the street to find 2 pirates patrolling. Before they can react, the guards grab them and pull them behind their cover.

"What are you vandals doing here? Who is leading you!?" Parm says with glaring eyes and a blaster pointed at their heads.

"We are here alone," says one of the pirates.
"We received a signal to come here and provide hel-" the other pirate elbows him and gives him a glance.

"Tell us who you are working for and we shall spare your lives." Parm says emotionlessly, "Take them back to the ship for advanced interrogation. If they scream you know what to do. Let's keep moving."

Their crew continues throughout the orb and finds a map left behind with the different loot available in the city, the center is circled with a bright red marker. *The interior is strong, but how long have they been here?*

"They are moving in to take the sacred seed, we must protect it at all cost." says Parm.
"Sacred seed?" asks Piza. *Sounds profitable!*
"Yes, the sacred seed is one of the last of its kind to begin producing vegetation above the ocean. Without it our hopes of returning to land might be lost forever." *I can't let that happen. I won't let that happen.*

"Call in the refugee ships and have them bring aid to the orbs on the outer quadrants. Bring in our guards to help secure the area and call me if you run into too much trouble. Alpha task force with me, we are going to the center."
"And me?" asks Piza.
"Yes, we might need a meat shield if things get tight."

The 10 of them take the clear cylinder elevator from the orb into the central hub of Samoa. As they enter the ship they are rudley smacked with the sounds of blaster shots, smog, and heat.

"The seed is located in the captain's vault on the first floor. Stay low and follow me." says Parm.

Crouched, they make their way through the docking bay into the 5th floor of the ship. They find 4 guards being pushed around by a dozen men in black suits.

"Your mommy ain't here to help you now." one man says as he slaps the crying guard's face to the ground. Several of the pirates give a sneering giggle.

In a whisper Parm says, "3.. 2.. 1.." her team jumps up from behind the crates and begins blasting the pirates to smithereens. 4 down, 8 down, 11 down. The last man alive begins crawling towards the elevator wincing in pain. Parm steps on the back of his knee, "Not so fast. Who brought you here?"

"It was Dronin from the Wake Island. He paid us to com-" Parm twists her foot on his knee and he lets out a shriek.

"Where is he now?" says Parm.
"They were headed to Captain's room a few hours ago!" the man coughs out.

Parm pulls out her blaster and shoots the pirate in the back of the head. "Let's move."

As the elevator descends, an alarm begins to sound in the ship. *They know we're here.* The elevator opens to find 20 burly pirates pointing their weapons at the door. A mid sized man with brown slicked back hair and three gold piercings on his left eyebrow steps forward, "What do we have here? The famed Parm of Honolulu. We've retrieved the seed, it's ours now."

"You have no idea what you are doing, where is the seed?" Parm says.

"I believe I should be the one asking questions here." says the pirate, "Should we kill you here where you stand? Or let the dogs have some fun?"

Parm makes a hand gesture behind her back, the belts of the crew explode froward massacring the pirates leaving them reeling on the ground.

"How.. What?" the leader croaks.

"Secure the seed. Scout the perimeter. We leave as soon as possible."

The team retrieves the seed pouch and approaches the elevator.

"Enjoy your time in hell." Parm says as the door closes.

 "This will send us all on a vacation to the Alps, or maybe India to have all the Octopus we can eat."

Piza and the Heroes Welcome and Personal Goodbyes

By Josh Eiermann

Cheers echoed through the halls as Parm and Piza arrived back at the main habitat. Parm was beaming while Piza looked uncomfortable. For someone that keeps to himself, introverted yet selfish, celebrating his accomplishments publically is awkward at best. He prefered to celebrate his hard work, alone, with himself as the primary recipient of the benefits.

"Isn't this great, Piza?! Doesn't it feel good to help out an entire community of people and be appreciated for it?"

"It sure does!" *not really.*

But they must leave each other.

However, as Piza saw the glow leaking from her skin, he couldn't help but think about how he might miss her. *She has this positivity about her that feels so genuine. It's nice to be around her. Her confidence is contagious.*

Syllble Writers

Josh Eiermann is an Economist at the BLS and holds a MSc in Applied Economics from Johns Hopkins University. Although he is published in peer-reviewed academic journals, this will be his first publication in fictional writing. Josh hopes to continue writing collaboratively and share his stories with the world.

David Russell's passion for creativity brings fun and enthusiasm to all of his projects. As a freshman at Florida State, he created a platform to help students buy and sell class notes online, Moolaguides.com. After achieving over $400,000 in revenue with over 20,000 users, he sold the business and traveled the world while producing the podcast Scale to Success. Now based in South Florida, David helps businesses develop their online presence through his consulting firm Let's Chat Marketing. For fun, he posts art on his Instagram page Frosencheeze, where he encourages friends and family to share their creations.

www.ingramcontent.com/pod-product-compliance
Lightning Source LLC
Chambersburg PA
CBHW021349060726
47591CB00006B/2240